THE
LONELY
PIGLET
IN THE GULLY

by

Albert Minwei Ai PHD

The Chinese University of Hong Kong

To order additional copies of this book, contact:
Xlibris
844-714-8691
www.Xlibris.com
Orders@Xlibris.com

ISBN: Softcover   978-1-6641-5823-8
        EBook   978-1-6641-5824-5

Print information available on the last page

Rev. date: 02/15/2021

THE
LONELY
PIGLET
IN THE GULLY

My ma raised three pigs, two adult ones in the pigsty and a piglet tethered near a pile of straw. I was seven years old at the time.

It's a happy time for me, following ma, to feed them, especially the piglet. He had pure white skin and two big ears, a teeny-weeny tail and four beautiful legs. Ma called him "Little Bit" as he was chubby and liked to roll around on the ground. Each time ma knocked on the wooden trough and said "Little Bit, it's time to eat", the straw pile would shake and break and our Little Bit would come out of it. He grunted with his small tail wagging.

Little Bit wolfed down everything, wobbled back, and hid himself again in the straw. The straw pile was his cocoon and he felt safe there. How lazy he was! Once I scratched his back, Little Bit would lie on the ground, close his eyes, and stretch the four legs. He really enjoyed it.

On sunny days, he liked to run on the farm land. Sometimes, pa freed him. On the land, pa and ma were digging sweet potatoes. I was collecting them into a basket. And Little Bit was running freely. Sometimes he might find a worm and played with it. Sometimes he might eat a sweet potato stealthily. When it was sunset, we went home together, following us like a shadow.

One day, ma found that there were red spots on Little Bit's skin. Something was going wrong. These tiny spots frightened us because an infectious disease was then spreading like a wild fire in the village and had killed hundreds of pigs.

To protect the other two pigs, ma and pa decided to send Little Bit away. I really didn't want that to happen but I could do nothing. Little Bit was left in a bamboo grove, which was about 15-minute-walk from our house.

For nights, I couldn't sleep. Lots of questions came into my head. I worried about him like a mother would for her child. Without the straw, where did he sleep? Was a there a wolf roaming in the dark? Or any other monster? I sobbed in the blanket. Many tears came out like raindrops from the sky.

The next day, ignoring ma's warning, I went to the bamboo grove with sweet potatoes in my pockets. In the bamboo grove, Little Bit saw me! Ran to me quickly, smelt my legs, wagged his tail again. I gave the sweet potatoes to him and watched him eating.

After a while, I was ready to leave. Little Bit ran after my heels. I dared not bring him home. But I also didn't want to leave him in the dark bamboo grove alone. I turned back and looked at him. He stopped and stared at me too.

Little Bit finally went home with me. When ma noticed him, she shouted and accused me of being thoughtless. If the other two pigs infected with the same disease, there would be no money for me to go to school. I cried loudly. Ma and pa were chasing him. The piglet was running and grunting.

I saw him hiding in the straw pile! How silly! The straw pile was quaking. Ma and pa surrounded it. Little Bit was caught and pulled out. He struggled and grunted, like a small rat caught in a trap.

This time, Little Bit was sent to a deep gully far away near a riverbank. He would never find the way home. I was so sad. Ma promised me to take him home if the spots on his skin disappeared. I was praying for that.

Each day, I went to see him and brought him a basket of vegetables and sweet potatoes. The gully was so steep that I couldn't get down and Little Bit couldn't climb up. At the bottom of the gully, there was a spring running out of the rock and flowing into the river. At least, he would not be thirsty. I threw the food to him from the top.

I also brought him his straw. Little Bit hid himself in it. When I called "Little Bit, it's time to eat", he would come out and grunt. However, several days later, Little Bit stopped the grunt and didn't show up.

Did he run away? He could not have climbed the steep wall of the gully. Did a big monster eat him? I saw no trace of any struggle. Thinking about the whereabouts of my piglet did not allow me to sleep peacefully for nights.

One day, ma returned and brought me a piece of happy news: the piglet was adopted by an old man! I knew that man, living on the top of a hill nearby. He took away my Little Bit. I was sad but also happy. The piglet had a new home!

I tried to visit him often. He was a happy piglet.

Printed in the United States
By Bookmasters